PUBLIC
LIBRARY
Sale of this book
supports literacy programs

THE PERFECT PET PAGEANT

Starring

PENNY LING

Written by Lisa Shea

Little, Brown and Company
New York Boston

This book is a work of fiction. Names, characters, places, and incidents are the product of the author's imagination or are used fictitiously. Any resemblance to actual events, locales, or persons, living or dead, is coincidental.

HASBRO and its logo, BLYTHE, LITTLEST PET SHOP, and all related characters are trademarks of Hasbro and are used with permission. © 2016 Hasbro. All rights reserved.

In accordance with the U.S. Copyright Act of 1976, the scanning, uploading, and electronic sharing of any part of this book without the permission of the publisher is unlawful piracy and theft of the author's intellectual property. If you would like to use material from the book (other than for review purposes), prior written permission must be obtained by contacting the publisher at permissions@hbgusa.com. Thank you for your support of the author's rights.

Little, Brown and Company

Hachette Book Group
1290 Avenue of the Americas, New York, NY 10104
Visit us at lb-kids.com

Little, Brown and Company is a division of Hachette Book Group, Inc. The Little, Brown name and logo are trademarks of Hachette Book Group, Inc.

The publisher is not responsible for websites (or their content) that are not owned by the publisher.

First Edition: May 2016

ISBN 978-0-316-38985-3

10 9 8 7 6 5 4 3 2 1

RRD-C

Printed in the United States of America

To Tippy, Figi, and Comet—
the best pets anyone ever had!

CONTENTS

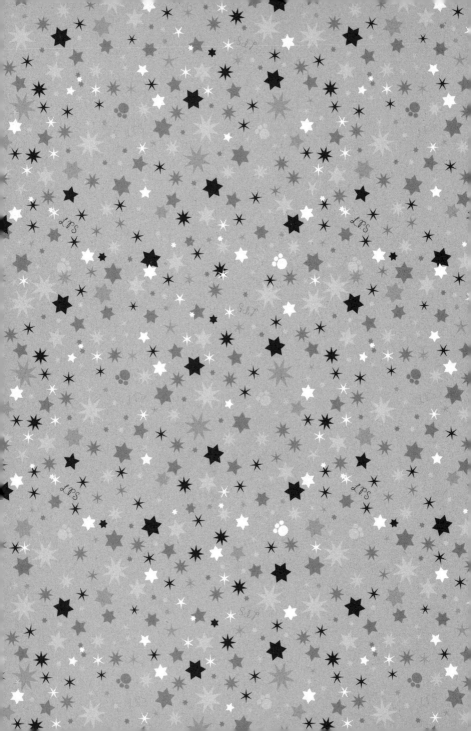

Chapter 1

"Minka, stop fidgeting," Blythe said to the cute pink spider monkey. "The Pet Pageant is only two weeks away, and I need to finish your outfit, plus all the other pets'."

Minka grinned. "I know, Blythe! But I'm just so excited about the pageant! And I love my new outfit!" Minka suddenly jumped away from Blythe to look at herself in a full-length mirror. "Ouch!" Minka yelped as she jumped.

"I told you to stop fidgeting," Blythe said again. "I was pinning the hem on your skirt when you jumped."

The two stood in front of the mirror together. "Oh, Blythe, it's just beautiful," Minka gasped.

"It did turn out pretty nice, if I do say so myself," Blythe agreed. Blythe's creation was a sky-blue sundress with straps that crisscrossed in the back.

Minka gave Blythe a hug. "You're the best designer in the whole world!" she cried.

Blythe laughed as she hugged Minka back. "And you're the sweetest spider monkey," she replied.

Ring-a-ling!

Everyone in the pet store turned to see who was at the door. It was Lewis, the neighborhood letter carrier, with a package for Blythe. He looked at Minka and Blythe hugging and smiled. "I've always read that monkeys are very affectionate creatures," he said. "I guess it's true."

"Oh, it's true all right," Blythe answered, with a quick glance at Minka to keep quiet. Blythe had a big secret—she could communicate with animals. And she wanted to make sure that her secret stayed a secret. While other people just heard barks, squawks, growls, chirps, and meows, Blythe heard actual words. She realized this talent was a great gift, and she didn't want to share it with the world. She was able to help the animals when they needed her, and they were able to help her, too. At first, Blythe found her ability a little scary, but now she wouldn't change things for the world.

Blythe looked down at the package Lewis handed her. "Oh, this must be the special fabric I ordered for the Pet Pageant," she said. "Thank you so much, Lewis!"

Just at that moment, Zoe came running over. "Did I hear you say 'special fabric'?" she asked. The Cavalier King Charles spaniel started pawing the package curiously.

Lewis couldn't hear what she said, of course. All he heard was a dog yipping excitedly and pawing at the package. "Well! Isn't she a nosy little thing?" Lewis said with a grin. "You'd almost think she knew what was in that package!"

"Almost," Blythe agreed. She waited until Lewis was gone to open the package.

Zoe sighed happily as she gazed at the bolts of soft silk and shiny satin. "Oh, I can't wait to see what you're going to use this for," she said.

"Don't worry, Zoe," Blythe assured her. "Even though you can't enter the Pet Pageant this year, I'm going to make you a new outfit, too."

Zoe gave a little pout. "Tell me again— why can't I enter this year?"

"Because you won last year," Blythe reminded her. "And were first runner-up the year before that. The judges decided it just wasn't fair to the other pets participating. You need to give some other pets a chance, Zoe," she said gently.

"I guess I can understand that," Zoe said with a sigh as she admired her reflection in a mirror.

Blythe laughed at Zoe looking at herself. "The Perfect Pet Pageant isn't all about beauty. The judges also consider the joy the pets bring to their owners, and their unique talents."

Zoe looked around at the pets in the pet shop. "We certainly have a lot of possible winners here," she said. "Since I can't compete this time, maybe I'll help mentor some of the pets. You know, give them tips on poise, beauty, and talent."

"That would be awesome," Blythe told her. "You're the most poised and glamorous pet I know!"

"Me too!" Zoe agreed. She looked around the pet shop, her eyes sparkling with excitement. "I can't wait to turn these pets into pageant stars!"

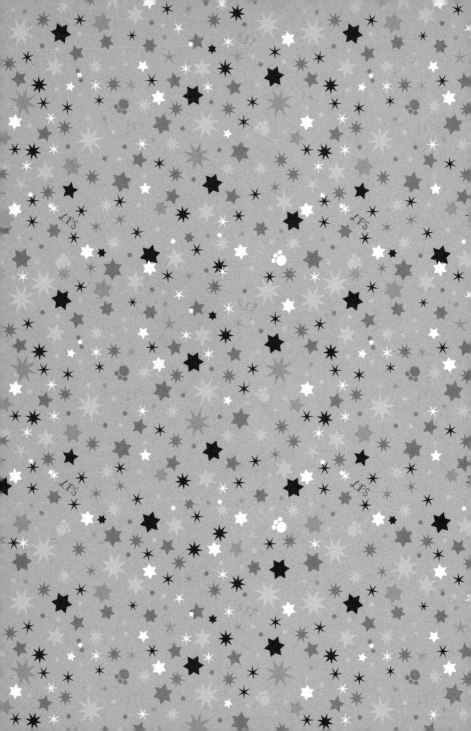

Chapter 2

Blythe decided to take all the pets to the beach for a day of fun in the sun, and also for some inspiration to finish up the outfits she was working on for the pageant. As the pets were frolicking in the surf and sand, Minka suddenly rushed over to Zoe's side. "Zoe, guess who's entering the Perfect Pet Pageant this year!" she squealed. "Guess!"

But before Zoe could answer, Minka held up a cell phone to show her. "Kitty Velvet!" she said dramatically.

Russell and Sunil came over to take a look. "Who's Kitty Velvet?" Sunil asked.

Zoe gasped. "Who's Kitty Velvet? She's only the most gorgeous feline on the face of the earth! She's a model, and has even appeared in some TV commercials." She showed the pets some photos of a beautiful black cat with a dramatic white stripe down her back. Zoe turned back to the pets. "Okay. In order to compete against Kitty, you guys are definitely going to need my help." Suddenly, her eyes lit on Penny Ling, who was tossing a disk on the beach with Pepper. Penny was panting as she chased after the disk. It was not so much that she was out of shape; it was just that pandas weren't used to running!

Zoe trotted over to Penny, who was sitting on the sand, taking a break. "Penny, I choose you," Zoe said dramatically. "I will be your mentor for the Perfect Pet Pageant! I think you have a lot of potential, but you need help with poise and grooming. But have no fear. By the time I'm through with you, people aren't even going to remember Kitty Velvet ever existed. I'm going to make you a *star*!"

Zoe waited for Penny to thank her and was surprised when Penny was silent. Penny was considering her options. She didn't even know if she really wanted to compete in a pageant—much less be a star! But suddenly, all the pets surrounded her.

"Let Zoe coach you, Penny," Pepper said. "We'll all still be in the contest because it will be fun, plus we all want to wear the new outfits Blythe is going to make for us. But at the same time, we'll all try to help you win!"

"Hooray for Penny!" Sunil shouted.

Penny still hesitated, but then Blythe came over. "I'll make you an extra-special outfit for the pageant," Blythe told her. "I know you don't like a lot of fuss, but I'll make you something very simple and elegant. I promise you'll love it!"

Still, Penny hesitated. "I'm not very good at being the center of attention," she said.

"That's what I'm here for, Penny!" Zoe said. "Please, let me help you!"

After a bit more hemming and hawing,

Penny grudgingly agreed to enter the pageant. All the pets cheered!

After all, Penny thought, *Zoe does know all about modeling and performing. How hard can being in a pageant be?*

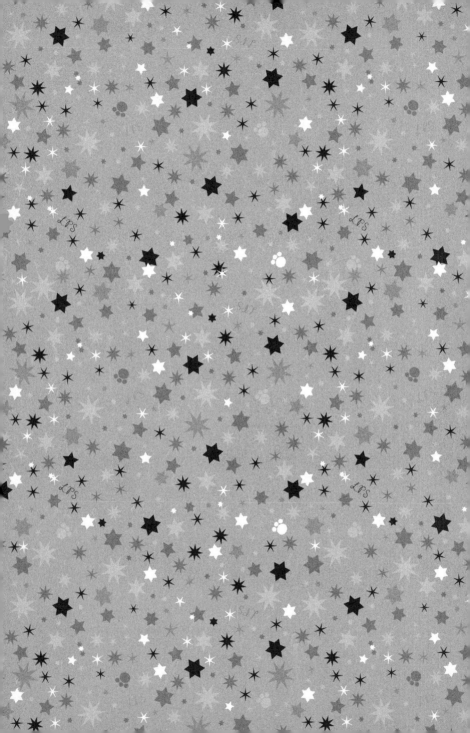

Chapter 3

Penny was having a wonderful dream. She was on a beautiful white sandy beach, sitting under a tree, looking out at the ocean. The water was sparkling, and she was eating a big bowl of bamboo shoots. The water was so soothing! The lapping waves seemed to be calling her name. *Penny...Penny... Pennnnnnyyyyyy!*

"PENNY!"

Penny was instantly wide-awake. And it wasn't the ocean calling her name, it was Zoe. Zoe was leaning over her and smiling. "Rise and shine, sleepyhead!" she said. "It's time to get you in shape for the Perfect Pet Pageant. And look who I've brought with me!"

Zoe leaned to one side, and Penny could see someone standing behind her. It was Jack LaLobster, personal trainer extraordinaire. "Hello, Penny," Jack said. "Do you remember me?"

Penny did remember Jack. He had tried to train her once before, with not-so-great results. "Yes, I remember you, Jack," she said. "Zoe, why—"

But Zoe wouldn't let her finish. "No time

to talk right now," Zoe said. "Exercise first; chat later!"

"Wait. What about breakfast?" Penny asked.

"You eat after the workout," LaLobster told her. "It's your reward for a job well done. Now give me fifty sit-ups, pronto."

Penny groaned. What a way to wake up! Next LaLobster made her jog in place, then do push-ups and squats. All the while, Zoe cheered her on. "You look great!" she'd sing out. "Go, Penny, go!" she cheered. When LaLobster finally said the workout was over, Zoe brought Penny a plate with one lone bamboo shoot on it.

"You call this a reward?" Penny complained, looking from Zoe to LaLobster who gently poked Penny in the stomach.

"When I see more muscle tone *here*," he said, "you'll see more *here*," pointing to the plate.

Penny groaned. Clearly, LaLobster didn't remember much from their first meeting. "Mr. LaLobster, don't you remember? I am in perfect shape for a panda. This is exactly the way our bodies are supposed to look. I'm supposed to be soft and cuddly, not... hard and...lobster-y."

"Penny, you are indeed in perfect shape for a panda," Zoe said earnestly. "But this is a competition. There will be lots of pets in good shape. We have to make sure you're in *even better* shape."

"It's hard to win a pageant," LaLobster agreed. "But don't worry, Penny. I've worked with many pageant pets in the past. And they always win! You want to be a winner, don't you?"

"Of course she does!" Zoe cheered. "Come on, Penny, ten more sit-ups! One... two... three... four... five..."

Penny got down on the floor and groaned again. *This pageant prep isn't going to be easy*, she thought to herself.

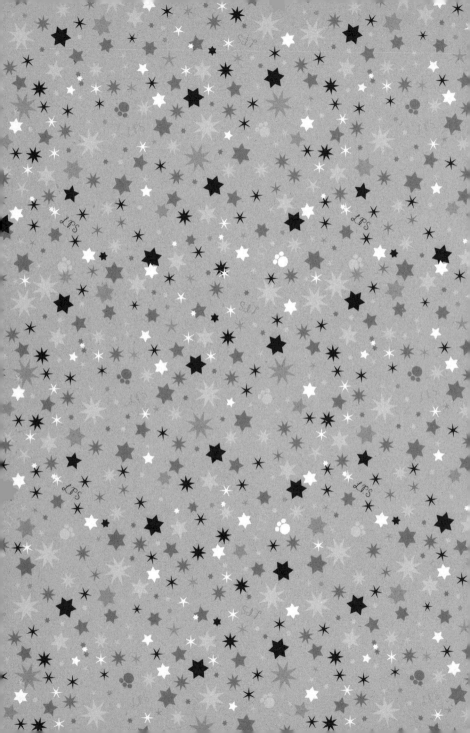

Chapter 4

The rest of the pets were starting to plan
what they would do for the talent portion
of the contest. Sunil was busy brushing
up on his magic tricks. He put on a black
top hat and stood in the middle of the pet
shop. "Hello, and welcome to the magic of
the Amazing Sunil!" he said. "I would like
a volunteer to help me. You, sir! Yes, you,

Mr. Green Gecko! Can you come over here, please?"

Vinnie walked over to Sunil with a big grin on his face.

"Please tell me your name, sir," Sunil said.

"Oh, knock it off, Sunil," Vinnie said. "You know my name is Vinnie."

"Just play along!" Sunil said in a loud stage whisper.

"Oh, okay. Hello, my name is Vinnie."

"Nice to meet you, Vinnie! Now pick a card, any card!"

Vinnie picked a card out of the deck. It was the queen of hearts.

"Okay. Please put your card back in the deck," Sunil said.

Vinnie put the card back.

"Now I will read your mind and tell you

your card," Sunil tells him. "Was it the ace of spades?"

"No."

"The two of clubs?"

"No."

"The three of diamonds?"

"No!"

"*Hmmm...*" Sunil said. "Then maybe it's this card...behind your ear!" He pulled a card out from behind Vinnie's ear with a flourish. It was the queen of hearts.

"Hey, that's pretty good," Vinnie said. "How did you do that?"

"I'm sorry, sir, a magician never reveals his secrets," Sunil told him.

Just at this point, Mrs. Twombly came by with a sack of pet food. She saw Sunil and Vinnie together.

"It just amazes me how all these creatures

get along," she said to herself, shaking her head as she walked to the back of the shop to put the food away.

Zoe was busy coaching Penny for the pageant. "You are a fabulous ribbon dancer, so that has to be your talent," Zoe told her.

Penny was thrilled. She loved ribbon dancing!

"Now, what kind of outfit do you want Blythe to make for you? Feathers? Sequins? Jewels? Lace? *Oooh!* Maybe something that lights up in the dark!"

Penny was dismayed. "Zoe, I don't want to wear anything like that," she said. "Especially when I dance. I want something easy and fun that I can move around in. Yes, it should be pretty, but it should also be simple. That's my style."

Zoe sighed. "That may work for every day, but not for a pageant," she said. "May I remind you I am the reigning perfect pet? Look what I wore last year." Zoe held up a photo of herself in an elaborate pink tutu adorned with sparkly silver stars. And she wore a matching pink sparkly headpiece.

Penny had to agree that Zoe looked fantastic. "Zoe, you were born to wear sequins and lace," she said. "That's your style. But like I said, that's just not me."

Blythe had been listening to this exchange. "Penny, I promise you, I will make you an outfit that is both outstanding and yet simple and chic at the same time. Nothing over-the-top."

Now it was Zoe's turn to be dismayed. "It has to be *a little* over-the-top, Blythe," Zoe said. "Remember, it *is* a competition."

"It will be fashionable but also comfort-able, simple, and chic," Blythe said firmly. "I always design with my client in mind. And in this case, my client is Penny."

"And that's why you're the best designer ever!" Penny squealed, and gave Blythe a big hug. "This is going to be the best pag-eant ever!"

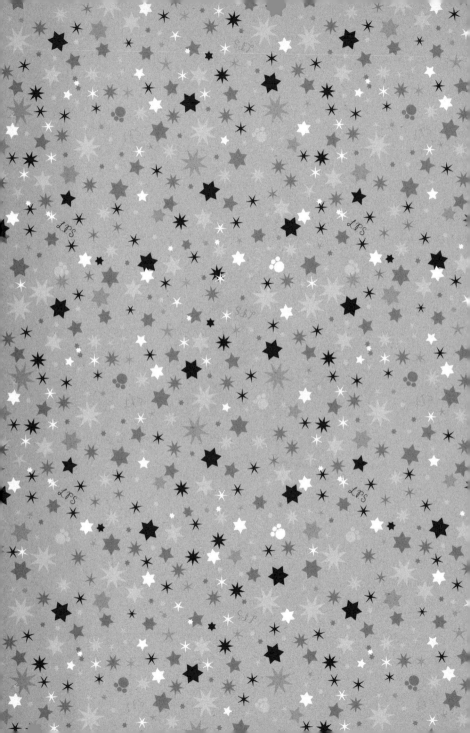

Chapter 5

All the pets were doing their best to try to give Penny tips on how to win the pageant.

"You need to show lots of enthusiasm and energy!" Minka said, jumping around the room.

"You need to smile more," Russell told her. "You have a great smile. Come on, smile for us." Penny gave the pets a sweet smile. "No, a *big smile*," Russell insisted. "Show some teeth. Sparkle! Smile with your eyes!"

"Smile with my eyes?" Penny said doubtfully. "What does that even mean?"

"Think of something that makes you really happy," Blythe said. "That will make your face light up."

Just then, Penny's stomach growled. "Bamboo shoots! A big bowl of bamboo shoots would make me really happy!" Penny cheered, and gave a wide, beautiful smile. All the pets laughed. Penny loved that her friends were trying to be helpful, and she was grateful for all their suggestions. She told them she'd try to remember all the tips, but in the end she would just have to be true to herself.

Suddenly, Pepper burst into the pet

shop, out of breath. "Paparazzi have been following me all morning," she explained. "They thought I was Kitty Velvet!"

"Paparazzi mistook you for Kitty Velvet? Feline model extraordinaire? I find that hard to believe," Zoe said.

"Well, they thought I was Kitty without makeup," Pepper explained. "And by the way, Zoe," she added indignantly, "some of them told me I looked a lot better!"

Penny reviewed the photos of Kitty Velvet online again. She had beautiful eyes and glossy black fur with that white stripe down her back, but pink nail polish on her claws and a feather boa around her neck. *Kitty tries really hard to look glamorous,* Penny thought to herself. *And she does look great. But in some ways, naturally pretty is just as good... maybe better.*

The next day, a dashing orange tom-cat arrived at the pet shop. Actually, Mrs. Twombly let him in. "The poor thing was outside the door whining all morning," she said. "I felt so bad for him, I just had to let him in. He must be hungry."

But the tomcat shocked everyone in the pet shop by rushing to Pepper's side. "*Mi amore!* My love! Good morning!" he said. "My name is Benny. When I saw you rushing away from the paparazzi yesterday, I fell in love. I knew there wasn't another cat in the world for me."

Pepper was startled. "I think there's been a misunderstanding here," she told him. "I'm not a cat...I'm a skunk."

Benny laughed heartily. "Beautiful *and* funny!" he said. "Oh, *mi amore*, how I adore you!"

Pepper sniffed the air. "What's that smell?" she asked. Then she laughed. "That's funny—that's what people usually ask me!"

"Ah! I brought you a little gift, my darling," Benny said, and gave Pepper a small stuffed toy filled with catnip. Pepper wrinkled her nose at the present. Benny kept lavishing compliments on Pepper. "Your fur...as dark as midnight...that beautiful white stripe down your back...those eyes that haunt my dreams!" But instead of being charmed, Pepper just kept getting more and more annoyed.

Mrs. Twombly watched the exchange between the two animals with amusement. Of course, she just heard the tomcat's wails and meows, but she also saw Pepper trying to avoid him. "Oh my, I do believe this tomcat is sweet on Pepper!" Mrs. Twombly exclaimed. "Isn't that the cutest thing you've ever seen?"

But by this time, Pepper couldn't take it any longer, and she asked Benny to leave.

Penny was surprised by Pepper's attitude. "A lot of creatures have issues with you because of your...aromas," Penny told her. "Here's someone who really likes you no matter what, and you're being so mean to him. And he seems really nice and could be a good friend. And you can never have too many friends!"

Pepper realized Penny was right, and she'd probably been too harsh with her admirer. "If he comes back, I'll be nice," she promised Penny. She looked out the pet shop window and realized she kind of liked the tomcat and his compliments. Would he ever come back?

Chapter 6

"Looking good, Penny! Just five more push-ups and you can take a break," Jack LaLobster said.

Penny really couldn't believe it. Was Jack LaLobster actually complimenting her? She took a deep breath and did the push-ups. "One...two...three... *OOF!*...four...five!" She sat up and gave a big sigh of satisfaction.

Suddenly, Zoe was by LaLobster's side. "Can I show her now, Jack? *Pleeeease?*"

"Oh, okay," LaLobster said. "Penny, get ready to be *dazzled!*"

Zoe pranced away and returned with a big box. "For me?" Penny said excitedly. She opened the box. Inside was a long, red sequined feather boa; red satin gloves; and a makeup kit. "For you to wear while you ribbon-dance in the pageant," Zoe told her. "Isn't it fabulous? And I told Blythe to match the red to the outfit she's making for you. And I'll help you do your makeup of course. I'm thinking big eyes and big lips!"

"Um, and I'm thinking *no.* No way," Penny told her. "Thank you very much, Zoe, but this is so not me."

"But it's a pageant," Jack LaLobster reminded her. "You're supposed to be a more glamorous version of yourself."

"Penny, I read today that Kitty Velvet is getting her outfits for the pageant designed in Paris! You know she's going to wear something magnificent. I just want you to be able to compete is all. Why don't you just give it a try?" She wrapped the feather boa around Penny's neck and handed her some ribbons to twirl. All the pets gathered around Penny to watch.

Penny started twirling the ribbons, but she wasn't very good. The feathers in the boa made her want to sneeze, the satin gloves made her arms itchy, and it was hard to concentrate on anything when she was starving!

"You can do it, Penny," Zoe said encouragingly. "I know it takes a little getting used to."

"You do look very glamorous, Penny," Pepper said.

"Like a movie star!" Sunil piped up.

"May I have your autograph?" Russell joked.

Looking at all her friends shining faces, Penny decided to give it a try. "Okay, I'll be a glamour girl for the pageant. But the minute it's over, Zoe..."

"Yes!" Zoe said, clapping her paws together. "That's all I ask, Penny! Just try!"

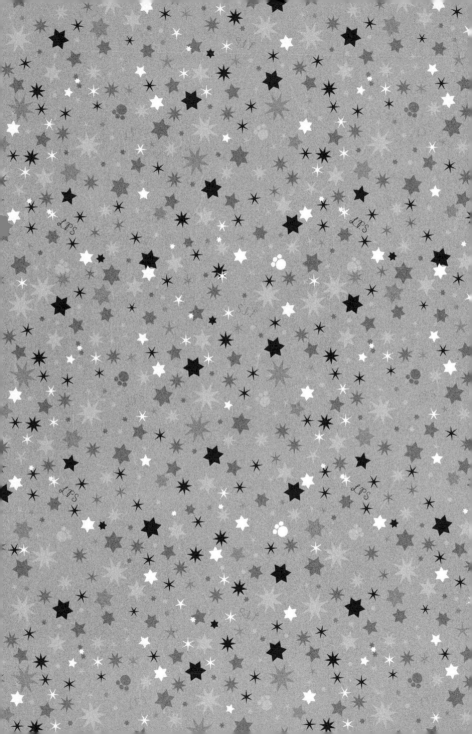

Chapter 7

The next day, Blythe presented all the pets with their outfits for the pageant. For Russell, an emerald-green pair of pants and jacket with slits in the back for his quills to show through. For Sunil, a gray silk suit with a jaunty bow tie. Pepper loved her lacy black dress with a big velvet bow for her fur. Minka loved her sky-blue sundress so much, it was hard to get her to take it off. Vinnie had a purple tuxedo! And even though Zoe wasn't in the competition, Blythe made her a fabulous hot-pink gown with gray satin along the hem and collar. But the crowning glory was a beach hat festooned with ribbons and sparkles and lace, and little round balls filled with glittery seashells. Blythe saved Penny's outfit for last. It was a simple red silk-shorts-and-tank-top combo, but she also had a beach hat—a beautiful ruby-red straw hat with a thick, red satin ribbon around the brim. Penny adored her outfit—it was both beautiful and simple at the same time. And she promised the pets she'd wear the gloves and feather boa for the talent competition.

"Let's go outside so you have more room to practice your ribbon dancing," Blythe said to Penny. "I want to see how the outfit looks while you move around."

Zoe and the pets agreed. They all went outside and watched as Penny practiced her ribbon-dancing routine. It started off okay, but as Penny started thinking about the pageant and imagining all eyes on her, suddenly she didn't feel quite so confident. She started fumbling around and getting her ribbons all tangled up in a ball.

The pets all tried to offer Penny advice.

"They say if you're nervous about public speaking or a performance, you should look for a friendly face in the crowd and concentrate on that person," Minka says. "Look for me, Penny!"

"Why should she look for you?" Zoe says. "She should look for me! Look for me Penny!"

It didn't take long for all the pets to start arguing among themselves about who was the best pet for Penny to focus on. They were so busy chattering, they didn't even hear the clicking of a camera or the rustling of a person hiding in the bushes. Once the pets were all back indoors, a man dialed a number on his phone.

"Hello, Priscilla? Claude here. I just found the most fabulous outfit for Kitty to wear in the pageant. It's perfect—a beautiful shade of deep ruby red. It's very simple yet elegant. We need to call Kitty's designer and send him this photo pronto. The pageant is just a few days away!"

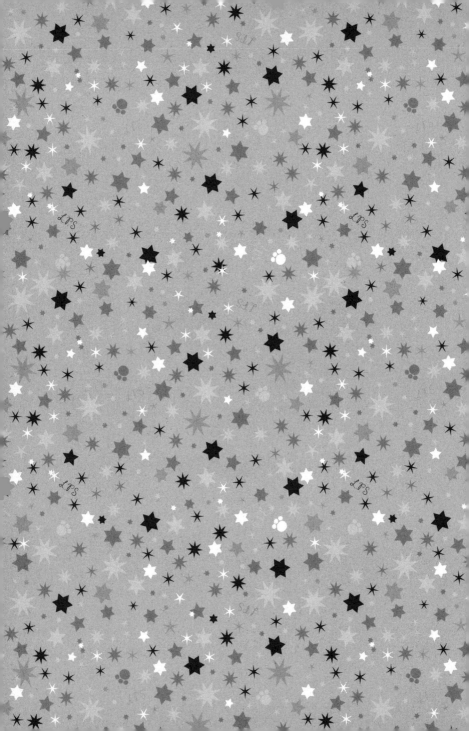

Chapter 8

The next couple of days were pretty quiet, as all the pets were working on their talent for the pageant. Minka decided she would create a painting the night of the contest, live in front of the judges. "It will be exciting—inspired!" she said.

Russell decided he would sing a song. "I will croon a romantic love song," he said.

"Perhaps some female hedgehog will hear me and fall in love." He walked up and down the length of the pet shop singing dramatically.

Although Pepper enjoyed doing stand-up comedy, she decided for a change of pace to perform a classical piano piece. She sat in front of a little keyboard and played a song from an Italian opera. Pepper played well, but the pets felt it was slow and dreary. Sunil tried to stifle a yawn but didn't succeed. Russell actually started dozing off, and Minka had to poke him awake.

"Can't you pep it up a little?" Vinnie asked. "Play something snappy, something people will want to dance to!"

"Yes! Something with a little pepper to it, Pepper!" Sunil said, and laughed at his own joke.

But Pepper refused to change her

selection. "I'm sure the judges will love it," she said. "What are you going to do, Vinnie?"

"I'm so glad you asked," Vinnie said. "Music, please, Sunil."

Sunil touched his cell phone and the song "Singin' in the Rain" started playing. Vinnie whipped out a tiny umbrella and started dancing. The umbrella was a little paper umbrella that once decorated a human's beverage glass. Vinnie twirled the umbrella as he danced. Even Pepper had to admit it was pretty cute.

Meanwhile, Penny's ribbon dancing was coming along beautifully. When she rehearsed for a second time in front of the pets, she made sure to focus on one pet as she twirled. One time she focused on Zoe, another time on Pepper, another time on Sunil, and so on.

"You look beautiful, and your ribbon

twirling is flawless," Zoe declared. "I'm so proud of you, Penny!"

"Thank you," Penny said. She was feeling pretty great. Her training with Jack LaLobster made her feel strong and helped her concentration and balance with her ribbons. And with her friends cheering her on, plus the beautiful outfit Blythe had designed for her, she started to think maybe being in a pageant wasn't so bad after all. "Meet this year's perfect pet winner—Penny," she said to herself. *It had a nice ring to it!*

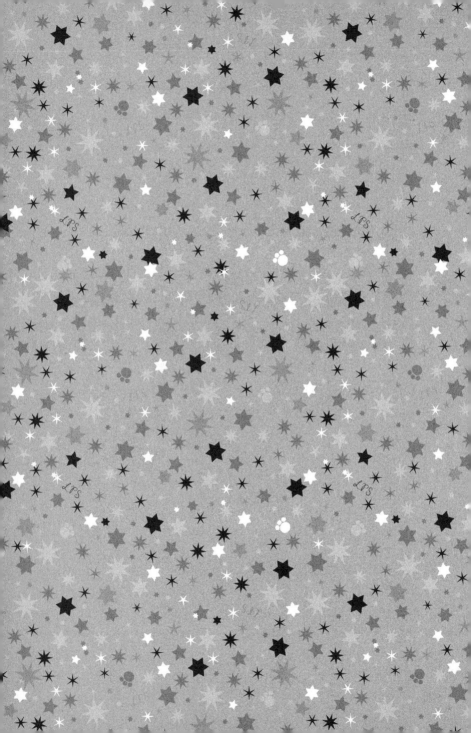

Chapter 9

The first thing all the pets saw the next morning was Benny the tomcat at the front door again. This time Blythe let him into the shop. He saw (and heard) Pepper playing the keyboard.

"My love, you never cease to amaze me," he said. "Funny, smart, beautiful, and now I must add talented to the list. You are truly the most wonderful cat in all the world!"

Pepper gave Benny an annoyed look and was about to say something when Penny caught her eye. Penny whispered, *"Be nice,"* and Pepper remembered that she shouldn't be mean to her biggest fan—even if he did think she was a cat!

"Benny, I don't know how more clearly to say this—I'm not a cat, I'm a skunk. The only thing I can think of to prove it to you is to spray you, and trust me, you do not want that!"

Benny was still not convinced. "My love, you could not smell more wonderful to me if you were standing in a garden of roses," he said. "I really can't believe there isn't a long line of suitors at this front door. You are so lovely—so much lovelier than that Kitty

Velvet everyone is always talking about. You are a hundred times prettier, just sitting there, than Kitty in her red feather boa and straw hat."

At these words, Pepper looked up with a start. "What did you just say? About Kitty Velvet's outfit?"

"I was saying that you look better than she does in her fancy clothes...Look!" Benny held up a cell phone and showed Pepper a photo of Kitty Velvet...and she was wearing a nearly exact replica of Penny's outfit for the pageant!

"Oh no! This is a disaster!" Pepper exclaimed.

Benny looked at the picture. "I agree the hat is a bit much, but the rest of the outfit I think is quite nice," he said.

"No! Not the outfit! I mean, yes, the

outfit, but, oh, never mind, it will take too long to explain." She handed the phone back to Benny. "Benny, I'm really sorry, but I can't chat with you right now. Can you please come back another time?"

"For you, my love, I will wait forever," Benny said as he left the pet shop.

Pepper rushed over to Blythe. "We have a problem," she told her. "Go online and do a search for 'Kitty Velvet, pageant outfit.'"

Blythe opened up her laptop and did a search. She gasped. "Oh *nooo*," Blythe said. "Someone must have taken a picture of Penny when she was rehearsing in her outfit and sent it to Kitty!"

"But there must be something we can do! Can't we sue them for stealing her outfit?"

Blythe studied the photo carefully. "Not really," she said. "They were very clever...

and sneaky! They changed just enough so it's not an exact copy of Penny's outfit. And they posted a photo right away so if anything, people will think *Penny* copied *Kitty*! No one will believe we had the original outfit."

Blythe called all the pets over to discuss the matter. She showed them the photo of Kitty Velvet wearing a nearly identical copy of the outfit she designed for Penny. The pets were shocked and dismayed.

"But you're the greatest designer in the world, Blythe," Zoe said. "I'm sure you can make something even more wonderful for Penny."

"I'll try," Blythe said. "But another problem is, I used up all the fabric I bought. So I don't have any really nice material left over for another outfit." She turned to

Penny. "But don't worry, Penny! I'll think of something!"

Penny was devastated. "Maybe it's not meant to be," she said sadly. "Maybe I shouldn't even enter the contest."

"Don't say that, Penny!" Blythe said. "I'll figure something out. I promise."

In the meantime, the pets had huddled into a group and were deep in discussion.

"What's going on with you guys?" Blythe asked.

Russell turned to Blythe, acting as the spokesperson for the group. "Blythe, we would all like you to take pieces of our outfits to make a new one for Penny," he said.

"It doesn't matter if our outfits are plain. We don't need to stand out," Minka agreed. "This pageant is all about Penny."

"What do you think, Blythe?" Zoe asked. "Do you think it would work?"

"Well, first of all, I think you all are the sweetest pets in the whole world to want to do this for your friend," Blythe said. "But I'm still not sure if I'll have enough material to make a whole new outfit, even if I take a little bit from each of you."

Just as Blythe and all the pets were considering this, Benny returned. As usual, he rushed immediately to Pepper's side.

"Hello, my love!" he said cheerfully. "I just couldn't stay away any longer. Do you have time now to chat?"

Pepper sighed. But then she remembered Penny telling her to try to be nice. "Hello, Benny," she said. "I really can't talk right now. I'm kind of in the middle of a crisis."

"What kind of crisis?" Benny asked. "Perhaps I can help."

"That's very sweet of you," Pepper said. "But I don't think you can. We need fabric for costumes for the Perfect Pet Pageant. And we need it right away. So unless you know somebody who works in a fabric store, or—"

At this point, Benny interrupted Pepper. "*Mi amore!* I can help!" he cried. "My owner is a seamstress. She always has tons of fabric in the house."

Blythe had been listening to the conversation. "Benny, that sounds great," she said. "But how do I approach her about this? What excuse do I even give for showing up at your doorstep?"

At this, Benny leaped into Blythe's arms. "My address is on my collar," he said. "Take me home. Tell her you found me, crying and hungry. She's always worried about me. I do run away a lot," he admitted. "Anyway, once you're inside the house asking about sewing, fabric should not be a problem! Come on! Let's go at once!"

Blythe agreed. "Well, it's worth a shot," she said. "Wish me luck!" she said to the other pets.

Benny snuggled into Blythe's arms. He looked back at Pepper contentedly. "I am going to be a hero for you, my love! I am going to save the day!"

Penny looked at Pepper and smiled. "What did I tell you, Pepper? You can never have enough friends. Go, Benny!" she cheered.

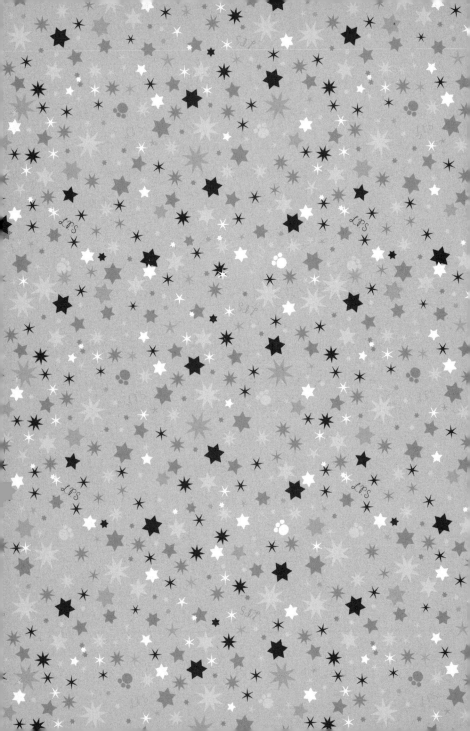

Chapter 10

Fortunately, Benny didn't live far from the pet shop. Blythe arrived at the address on Benny's collar and rang the doorbell. A sweet, gray-haired little old lady answered the door. "Yes?" she asked, and then looked down. She saw Benny in Blythe's arms. Benny let out a long wail and stretched out his front paws.

"Benny!" the woman cried. "Oh, I've been so worried about you!" Blythe quickly handed Benny over.

"He's fine," Blythe said. "I found him wandering in front of the pet shop where I work. I gave him a little something to eat, and then noticed his tags, and brought him right back here."

"Oh, I can't thank you enough!" the woman said. "Come in, dear, come in! My name is Sarah."

Blythe followed. "My name is Blythe," she said.

Blythe immediately noticed a huge sewing machine in the front room. "Oh my! What a beautiful sewing machine," she said. "Do you sew a lot?"

"Why, yes, dear, I'm a seamstress. I make all my own clothes," Sarah said proudly.

"I love to sew, too," Blythe told her. "As a matter of fact, I'm in the middle of a sewing project right now, and I'm in a bit of a dilemma. I ran out of fabric and—"

Before Blythe could even finish the sentence, Sarah took her by the hand. "Oh, my dear, please follow me!" She took Blythe into a small room filled with mannequins and boxes of fabric, buttons, lace, and ribbons. "I always buy more than I need. If there's anything here that can help you with your project, please help yourself! Consider it a reward for bringing back my darling Benny."

Benny purred contentedly in Sarah's arms, then turned to look at Blythe and gave her a big wink!

Blythe looked through the boxes and found the perfect fabric—it was a deep sapphire-blue satin. *Penny will love this,* Blythe thought to herself. And then she had another idea—she'd trim the outfit using pieces from the other pets' costumes—so it will be like they all had a part in creating Penny's look.

Blythe told Sarah about the Perfect Pet Pageant. "It sounds wonderful!" Sarah exclaimed. Then she looked at Benny. "Why, I think I'll enter Benny in the pageant!" she cried. She gave Benny a hug. "Won't that be fun, Benny-kins?"

Benny looked at Blythe, alarmed, and let out a yowl.

"*Oooh,* listen to him! I think he's excited!" Sarah exclaimed.

All Blythe could do was laugh. "'Excited' isn't the word for it!" she said.

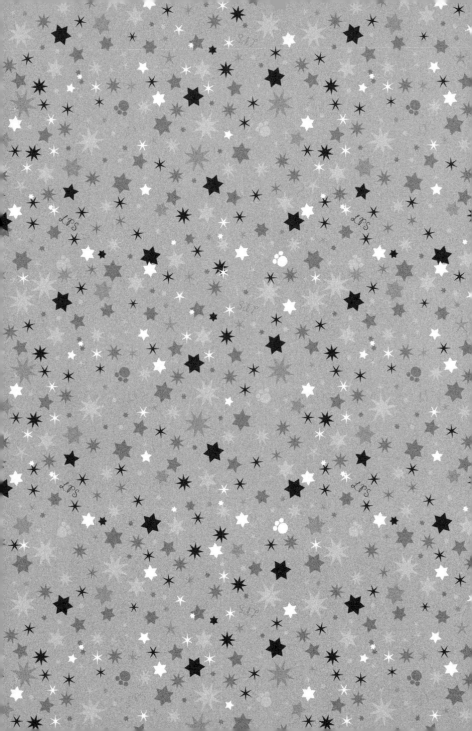

Chapter 11

"No, no, no, Penny, you're still not doing it right! Pay attention!" Zoe was trying to give Penny some pageant tips, and things weren't going very well. "Now watch," Zoe said. "Pretend I'm walking down a runway." Zoe walked slowly, turning her head first to the left, then to the right. She batted her lashes, smiled, tossed her head back, and laughed.

"What are you laughing at, Zoe?" Penny asked.

"Nothing," Zoe said. "I'm just laughing so the photographers can take a picture of me that shows off all my beautiful white teeth."

"*Ohhh,*" Penny said. "I see."

"Okay," Zoe said. "Now you try."

"All right," Penny agreed. She took a deep breath and began walking slowly. She tried batting her eyelashes the way Zoe had, but she just looked like she was blinking really hard. She forced out a hearty laugh. "Ha-ha-ha!" Penny said.

Zoe looked at her, annoyed. "What was *that*?" she asked.

"Well, it's hard for me to fake laughing," Penny said. "I feel really uncomfortable doing it."

Minka had been watching this exchange. "You know, Zoe, what works for you may not necessarily work for Penny," she said. "You really shouldn't force her to do anything she doesn't want to."

"You don't understand," Zoe replied. "I'm her mentor. Penny knows anything I tell her to do is for her own good. Isn't that right, Penny?"

"Well..." Penny hesitated.

"Well? Well what? Why are you hesitating?" Zoe demanded.

"Well, Minka has a point," Penny said. "You are being...kind of bossy, Zoe."

"There! You see?" Minka said triumphantly. "I knew it!"

"You knew what? How to cause trouble? Look, Minka, things were going just fine until you butted in."

"I don't think so, Zoe," Minka said. "I think Penny has probably been unhappy for quite a while. She's just too nice to say anything."

Zoe whirled around to look at Penny. "Is this true?" she demanded. "You simply cannot be my protégé, and I cannot be your mentor if this is how you feel. And you can't take Minka's side, either. You either agree with me and trust that I'm teaching you with the best intentions at heart, or you agree with Minka. And if you agree with Minka, we can't be friends. You're either with me or against me, Penny. You have to choose!"

Penny felt tears well up in her eyes. "Don't make me choose...I can't. You're both my friends!"

"Well, then, I'll make it easy for you," Zoe

replied. "I am no longer your mentor!" And with that, Zoe flounced off.

"*Nooo...*" Penny wailed. Now what was she going to do?

Later that day during lunch, Sunil and Vinnie were discussing the situation.

"Well, I can see Zoe's side during this," Sunil said. "I mean, Penny did agree to have Zoe as her mentor."

"But I can see Minka's side," Vinnie told him. "I mean, Zoe can be really bossy, and a lot of what she wants Penny to do is not her style at all."

"But that's the point," Sunil said. "Zoe is training Penny to compete in a pageant. She's not supposed to be herself."

"Why are you always so stubborn?" Vinnie said. "Can't you even consider my point of view?"

"Can't you even consider mine?" Sunil cried. "Some friend you are!"

"Don't talk to me!"

"Fine! Don't talk to me, either!"

Pepper bounced into the room. "Hey guys, what's going on?" she asked.

"Oh, be quiet, Pepper!" Vinnie yelled.

"Yeah, just leave us alone," Sunil said.

"Hey!" Pepper said, confused. "What's going on?"

Russell had been observing all this quietly. *Uh-oh*, he thought. *I'd better fill Blythe in on what's been going on around here.*

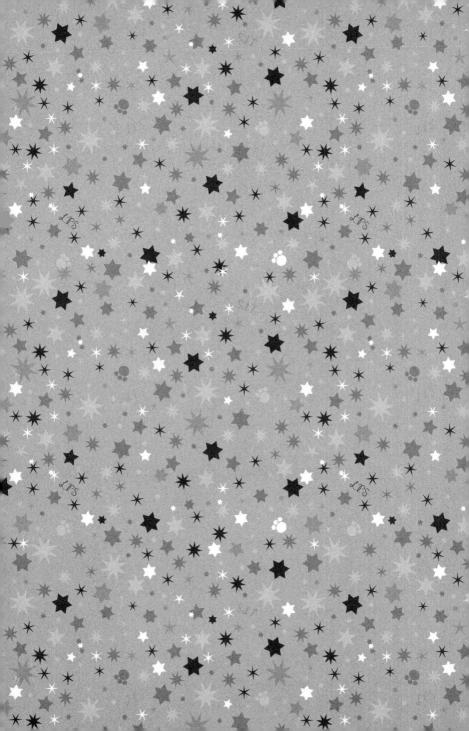

Chapter 12

"And so that's what's been going on," Russell said. He'd told Blythe all about the pets arguing. "Basically, everyone is mad at each other."

"This is terrible!" Blythe said. "And the pageant is just a few days away. We have to get everyone speaking to each other again."

Blythe had finished everyone's outfits for

the pageant, so she figured maybe if everyone tried them on, that would get them speaking to each other again.

And it did—only not in the way Blythe hoped!

Zoe tried on her pink gown. She looked and felt beautiful until Minka muttered, "Pink is a very sweet color. Too bad in this case it doesn't match the personality of the person wearing it."

"I...am...as sweet as pie," Zoe said indignantly. "Just ask anybody. As for you...well, I get a little seasick looking at all that blue."

"Hey!" Blythe said, upset. "I made that sundress, Zoe!"

"Oh, the craftsmanship is outstanding, Blythe," Zoe told her. "It's just too bad that you don't have a better model to show it off."

Sunil was admiring himself in a full-length mirror when Vinnie walked by and coughed, "Goofball in a goofy bow tie!"

"Who ever heard of a purple tuxedo?" Sunil sneered.

"Okay, this has got to stop," Blythe said. "The pageant is coming up very soon, and you guys have to all make up and make nice or else…"

"Or else what, Blythe?" Zoe asked. "It's obvious we aren't going to be friends anytime soon."

In order to break the tension, Russell turned on the TV. As he was flipping channels, he noticed a celebrity reporter talking about Kitty Velvet. He turned up the volume so all the pets could listen. "I met with Kitty Velvet's owner today," the reporter was saying. "And I have to say, she is pretty confident about Kitty winning the Perfect

Pet Pageant. When I asked her about it, she said there was no doubt in her mind Kitty was going to take the top prize. 'Kitty is more beautiful and talented than any pets around here,' her owner told me. 'I mean, who is the competition? A goofy dancing gecko? A silly panda waving her silly ribbons? This pageant is going to be a piece of cake for Kitty.'"

All the pets were silent for a moment.

"We've been so stupid," Pepper said.

"We've forgotten the whole point of the pageant…we wanted Penny to win because we love her," Sunil said.

"And here we are all fighting and making everything worse for her," Zoe added.

"And she's always saying stuff about how friendship is so important and you can never have enough friends... *Ooooh,* I feel terrible." Russell groaned.

"And that stupid Kitty Velvet thinks she's going to win!" Vinnie fumed. "Goofy dancing gecko indeed!"

"Well, first things first," Sunil said. "First, we apologize to one another. Then we have to find Penny and apologize to her. And third, we make sure Penny has all our support and kicks that Kitty Velvet's butt!" He turned to Vinnie. "I'm sorry, buddy."

"Aw, I'm sorry, too, Sunil."

But Zoe and Minka weren't looking at each other.

"Zoe? Minka? Don't you two have something you want to say to each other?" Blythe asked.

Still, there was nothing but silence between

the beautiful Cavalier King Charles spaniel and the spider monkey.

Pepper broke the silence.

"Oh, for goodness' sake. Zoe, Minka, both of you! Say you're sorry! DO IT FOR PENNY!"

Those words seemed to wake the two pets up. Suddenly, they couldn't say they were sorry fast enough.

"I shouldn't have questioned your mentoring skills," Minka said. "I'm so sorry, Zoe!"

"I can be a bit bossy," Zoe admitted. "I need to learn to be a better listener, especially when my friends are concerned. I'm sorry, too, Minka!" The two pets hugged.

"Okay, next, we need to apologize to Penny," Sunil said.

Penny was in bed, under the covers,

sobbing. All the pets sat in a circle on the top of the bed.

Blythe spoke up. "Penny, everyone is here, and they all want to speak with you."

At this, the sniffling grew softer, and then finally, two large gray eyes appeared over the blanket. "What do you want?" Penny asked.

Russell decided to be the spokesperson of the group. "Penny, we're sorry. We all got so wrapped up in how we thought things should go, we forgot about the most important person here—*you*!"

"Penny, you should act in the pageant however you want," Zoe said. "And I will support you two hundred percent. I love you!"

"We all love you, Penny," Minka said. "Can you ever forgive us?"

"Well…" Penny hesitated, but only for a moment. "Of course I can! You guys are my best friends. I forgive you!"

"Fantastic," Vinnie cheered. "Now it's time to kick some pageant butt!"

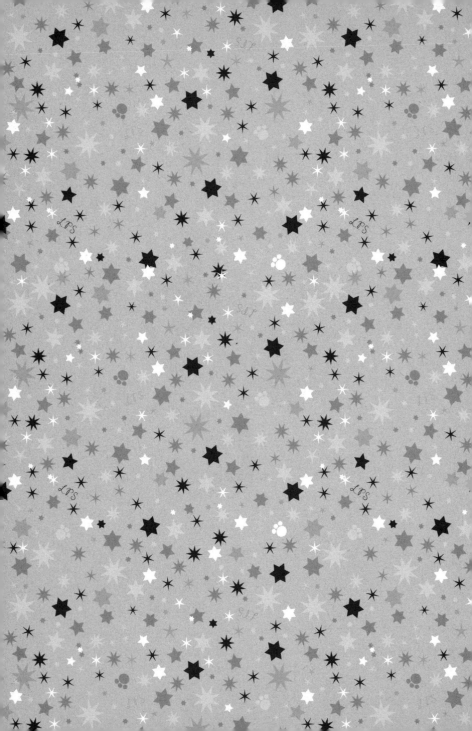

Chapter 13

The Perfect Pet Pageant was getting a lot of publicity because of Kitty Velvet. Reporters were stopping pet owners all over the city, asking them if they were entering their pets. One night Blythe was watching the news, and she saw Sarah, Benny's owner, being interviewed.

"Pepper, look, it's Sarah!" Blythe said.

Sarah was holding Benny and petting him. Benny didn't look very pleased.

"Excuse me, ma'am, but I was wondering if you're entering your cat in the Perfect Pet Pageant?" the reporter asked.

"Oh yes! I'm looking forward to it," Sarah said. "This will be the first time I've ever entered Benny in any sort of contest."

"And what will Benny do for the talent portion?" the reporter asked. "What is Benny good at?"

"Oh, I haven't decided on that yet," Sarah said. "Running away from home? He's very good at that!" And Sarah and the reporter both laughed.

At this point, Benny looked right into the camera and meowed loudly. Sarah and the reporter just laughed again because all they heard was a cat meowing. But in the Littlest

Pet Shop, Blythe, Pepper, and all the pets heard, "Pepper, my love, I miss *youuuuu*!" All the pets cracked up.

The pets decided it was time to brush up on their talents. Minka had been practicing her on-the-spot paintings. So far she'd painted bananas, a bowl of grapes, and more bananas.

"Shouldn't you paint something a little more exciting than bananas?" Sunil asked.

Minka shrugged. "I'm a monkey. People will expect me to paint bananas," she said. "Give the people what they want, that's what I always say."

Vinnie was practicing his "Singin' in the Rain" number. He hopped around gracefully and twirled his umbrella. "Blythe, this would be so much better if I had tap shoes," he said. "Can't you find me a pair?"

"Vinnie, there are no such thing as gecko-sized shoes, much less tap shoes," Blythe told him. "You'll just have to do without."

Sunil was trying to convince Vinnie to help him out with his magic act. "I need someone to saw in half," he begged. "Every great magician does it in his act."

"And the key words there are 'great magician,'" Vinnie said. "You want me to let you—an amateur magician at best—saw me in half? No, thank you. I'll pick a card, I'll hold your top hat while you pull a rabbit out of it, but using dangerous tools on my body is where I draw the line."

Russell was singing his love song. He closed his eyes and sang passionately, with all his heart. When he opened his eyes again, he saw all the pets had their hands covering their ears. "Oh dear," he said. "I guess I'm not as wonderful a singer as I thought?" He looked over at Blythe for help.

"Maybe another type of romantic performance?" Blythe suggested. "If you can't sing a romantic song, maybe recite a romantic poem instead?"

"That's a great idea, Blythe!" Russell said. "I'll recite a romantic poem. An original poem—one I that I will write myself! What rhymes with love? Love...dove... glove...blue sky above...Hey, I'm a poet and now I know it! Ha!" He hurried off in search of a pencil and paper.

Pepper sat down at the keyboard to play her opera piece. But after the first few notes, she stopped. "Playing this song makes me think of Benny," she said. "I miss him!"

The only pet who didn't seem to need

any practice was Penny. She gracefully twirled her ribbons like a pro. Everyone stopped to admire her.

"Penny, when you twirl those ribbons, you are poetry in motion," Sunil said admiringly.

"Thank you," Penny said. She was getting more and more excited about the pageant as the days went on. She felt super confident, her friends weren't fighting anymore, and Blythe was making her a beautiful new outfit. Even Jack LaLobster pronounced her in "perfect pageant shape" during her last workout.

Blythe walked over to Penny holding a box. "I've finished your outfit for the pageant, Penny," she said. "And I have a little surprise for you." Instead of a feather boa, Blythe made Penny a multicolored scarf with pieces of fabric from all the pets' costumes. There was a little black lace from Pepper's outfit, a bit of sky blue from Minka's dress, gray silk from Sunil's suit, and deep purple from Vinnie's tuxedo. But the best part? Blythe took a few of the sparkly seashell balls from Zoe's straw hat and put them on Penny's.

"So when you're performing, remember you're going to be carrying a little piece of all your friends with you," Blythe said. "So there's no reason to be nervous or scared. All the while you are onstage, you will be covered in your friends' love."

"Wow. I'm not usually into sappy, but that's just beautiful, Blythe," Zoe said.

"It's beautiful because it's true," Minka said.

"Penny, there's no looking back now,"

Sunil said cheerfully. "You've got everything you need to succeed!"

"What do you think, Penny?" Russell asked her.

"Let the games begin!" Penny said. "I'm ready!"

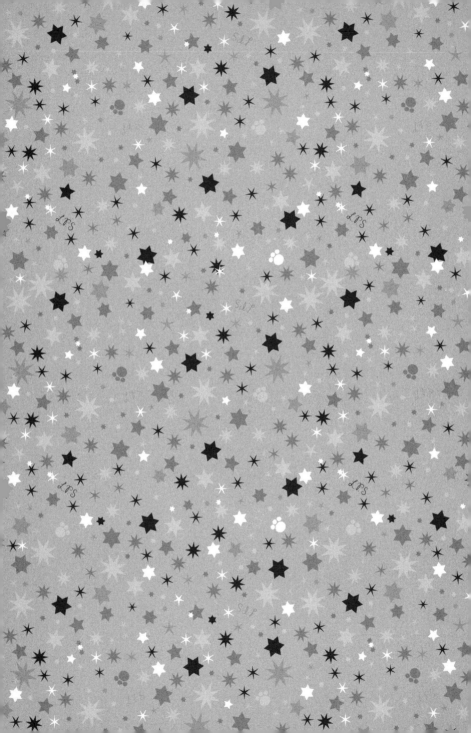

Chapter 14

The big day was finally here! The boardwalk was packed with people, pets, and reporters and photographers. Amid the crowd, Blythe spotted the Biskit twins, who somehow managed to look excited and bored at the same time. The girls saw Blythe and made their way over to her.

"Hello, Blythe. Is she here?" Whittany asked.

"Is who here?" Blythe said.

"Oh, come on," Brittany said. "Kitty Velvet. She's the only reason we're here. She's the only reason anyone who's anyone is here!"

"I don't know about that," Blythe said. "I'm pretty excited about entering my pets."

"Of course you are," Whittany said. "We know one of your little dogs won last year, but that was before there was any real competition."

Zoe heard this and started growling.

"Come on, Whittany," Brittany said. "She's not here yet, and this is boring. Pets bore me."

"Your father owns a pet shop!" Blythe said, confused.

"What-ever," Whittany said with a shrug. "See you later."

Benny the tomcat had escaped from his owner, again, to see Pepper.

"My love, you are here!" he said happily.

"Hello, Benny," Pepper said with a laugh. "Don't you look nice!"

Benny was decked out in a black tuxedo. He sighed. "Sarah made me wear this, of course," he said. "I am not really the tuxedo type. But it's just one more thing I will endure to see you again!"

"Benny! There you are!" Sarah was suddenly between them. Sarah looked at Blythe. "Hello, dear," she said as she scooped Benny up. "I said his biggest talent is running away. Well, good luck to you and all your lovely pets!"

"And good luck to you and Benny," Blythe said.

Mrs. Twombly hurried over to Blythe. "Blythe, they're just about to begin," she said. "We need to line everyone up."

"Don't worry, Mrs. Twombly, I'll take care of it," Blythe said. When Mrs. Twombly was out of earshot, she said to the pets, "Okay, everyone, this is it!" All the pets wiggled and giggled with excitement as they lined up in front of her.

Suddenly, there was a flurry of cameras clicking. "There she is!" someone yelled, and Blythe and all the pets turned in the direction of the voice.

A stretch limo had pulled up to the beach. A chauffeur opened up a door, and out stepped a very fashionable young woman walking a cat on a leash. The cat was Kitty

Velvet, and she was wearing the ruby-red outfit Blythe had originally designed for Penny. Kitty Velvet walked slowly and turned every time she heard a camera click or someone yelled, "Kitty! Over here!" She smiled and purred and batted impossibly long lashes.

"Fake eyelashes," Zoe muttered under her breath.

"Don't worry, Penny," Minka told her. "Your new outfit is even better than the one Kitty stole from us. And you're real, and she's just a big fake!"

"Thank you, Minka," Penny said. Truth be told, Penny was a little nervous. Kitty Velvet seemed so cool, calm, and collected. Would Penny be able to hold her own against her in the pageant?

Everyone applauded as all the pets and their owners got in line. What a lineup!

Fur and feathers as far as the eye could see. There were colorful birds, fluffy bunnies, lizards, geckos, dogs, cats, hedgehogs, hamsters, monkeys, and one very nervous panda.

The master of ceremonies, Gerry Geralds, walked up to a microphone to start the pageant. "Greetings, everyone, and thank you for coming out for our fifth-annual Perfect Pet Pageant. I'm your host, Gerry Geralds, and we're going to have a great time today, aren't we?" Everyone cheered. "All right, then! We will first have our contestants walk down the runway with their owners so the judges can get a better look at them. Pets, it's your turn to shine! Go for it!"

Some of the pets raced down the runway. One puppy even peed on it! One angry cat hissed at everyone the entire way down. Blythe and Mrs. Twombly walked behind their pets, knowing they would be well behaved. Minka loved it—she bounced down the runway, waving at the crowd. "Isn't she cute?" kids whispered to one another, and snapped photos of Minka with their phones. Sunil was a little shy and kept his eyes downward the entire time. Pepper was a bit nervous and started to let out a bit of an aroma, but was able to keep it under control. Russell stayed close to Blythe, and Vinnie was a natural ham, stopping to pose every few minutes.

But the real surprise was Penny! She strutted down the runway as if it was the most natural thing in the world. She looked out into the audience and saw Jack LaLobster nodding at her. "Smile!" Jack yelled. "Smile with your eyes!" Penny remembered when Russell said that to her! She thought of a big plate of bamboo shoots and gave everyone a beautiful smile.

"*Oooh*, that panda is so adorable," one little girl sighed. "Can we take her home, Mommy?" Everyone was in love with Penny!

Next up was Benny with his owner, Sarah. Benny was so uncomfortable in his little tuxedo. He kept pawing at the bow tie by his neck, which everyone thought was hilarious. "The things I do for love," Benny muttered to himself. Then he caught Pepper's eye and gave her a big wink!

Just then, a murmur went through the crowd. Kitty Velvet was gliding down the runway, purring loudly. Her glossy black fur with that unique white stripe, her huge green eyes—you couldn't help staring at the magnificent cat. She paused at the end of the runaway and sat prettily for a moment, the better for everyone to take her photo.

"She's so cool," Whittany whispered to her twin, Brittany. "It was totally worth it to come down here just to see her."

"Totally," Brittany agreed.

After all the pets had taken their walk, Gerry Geralds walked to the microphone again. "Now that we've seen all the pets, the next step will be to talk to their owners and find out a little more about them all. Won't that be fun?" The crowd applauded. "All right, then! He consulted a list. Our first pet up will be...Russell Ferguson with Blythe Baxter."

"Okay! We're on!" Blythe whispered to Russell.

"Hello, Blythe! My, this is a fine-looking porcupine you've got there," Gerry said.

"Grrr..." Russell growled quietly.

Blythe smiled politely. "Russell is not a porcupine, Gerry. He's a hedgehog."

"A hedgehog! What's the difference?" Gerry asked.

"Grrr..." Russell growled again, this time a bit louder. He hated being mistaken for a porcupine!

"Well, unlike porcupine quills, a hedgehog's quills are not barbed, and they're not poisonous," Blythe said. "And the inside of the quills are mostly hollow, which makes them light, but strong!"

"Fascinating!" Gerry said. "And why would you say Russell the hedgehog is the perfect pet, Blythe?"

"Russell is very loyal," Blythe said. "He's very devoted to me, and keeps me company in the pet shop where I work. He's very sweet and smart, and hedgehogs eat pesky insects, which is a very good thing!"

"Indeed it is!" Gerry said cheerfully. "Okay, audience, let's hear it for Russell the hedgehog!" The audience applauded politely.

"Next up we have Sarah Shaw and her cat, Benny," Gerry said.

Sarah and Benny walked over to Gerry. Benny was scowling and tugging at his collar.

"*Awww,* someone looks like he doesn't want to be here," Gerry said.

"Oh, but I'm so glad he's here!" Sarah said. "Benny is my best friend. He brings so much happiness and excitement to my life. I don't know what I'd do without him."

"Well, that certainly sounds like a potential perfect pet, doesn't it, ladies and gentlemen?

Let's hear it for Benny!" Once again the audience applauded.

"Okay, next up we have Blythe and Sunil! Hello again, Blythe!"

"Hello again, Gerry. I'll be up here a lot because I work in a pet shop," Blythe explained.

"And tell me about your little weasel there, Sunil."

"Weasel?" Sunil said, insulted. But except for Blythe, the other people just heard an indignant squeal. Everyone laughed!

"Sunil isn't a weasel," Blythe said patiently. "He is a mongoose. And he's wonderful. He may seem quiet and shy, but did you know a mongoose can kill a snake?"

"No, I did not know that! Seems like a good little guy to have around. Thank you,

Blythe and Sunil! Next up we have Vinnie and Mrs. Twombly."

Mrs. Twombly walked over to Gerry, holding Vinnie. "Tell me about your little lizard friend, Mrs. Twombly," Gerry said.

"Well, this here is Vinnie," Mrs. Twombly said. "He is a gecko. He's not as cuddly as some other types of pets, but he's a wonderful dancer, as you soon shall see!"

"I can't wait!" Gerry said. "Thank you, Mrs. Twombly. Who do we have next? Why it's our friend Blythe again...with Pepper... the...now, this time I hope I'm wrong! Is Pepper a skunk?"

"Indeed she is, Gerry," Blythe said. From a far corner of the boardwalk, Benny gasped.

"Don't listen to them, my love!" Benny

yelled. But all anyone heard was a cat yowling.

"Is it...safe to have Pepper here in a pet contest, Blythe?" Gerry asked.

"Of course," Blythe said. "She doesn't spray unless she's upset or angry."

"And you're not going to make me angry, are you, Gerry Geralds?" Pepper asked, looking up at Gerry with an evil gleam in her eye. Gerry was uncomfortable.

"*Hmmm*...I don't like the way she's looking at me," Gerry said. "Let's move on."

A few other pets and their owners were introduced. Minka kept fidgeting.

"Minka, calm down," Blythe said. "You're making me nervous!"

When Gerry announced Minka's and Blythe's names, Minka bounded right over to Gerry.

"Well, hello, Minka! It's nice to meet you!" Gerry said.

"Minka is very bubbly and friendly," Blythe said. "That's one of the reasons I think she's the perfect pet!"

"She certainly is adorable," Gerry agreed. Suddenly, Minka leaped onto his head!

"Hey!" Gerry shouted.

Blythe giggled. "I'm sorry, Gerry," she said. "I guess she thinks you're a tree!" Everyone laughed as Blythe said, "Come down now, Minka," and Minka jumped into her arms.

"Now, next up we have a cat. But not just any cat. This cat needs no introduction. So why am I introducing her? Ha-ha-ha. Everyone, meet Kitty Velvet and her owner, Priscilla Lee."

"About time," Whittany Biskit muttered,

and got her cell phone ready to snap a picture.

Everyone gasped in awe as Priscilla held up Kitty for the crowd to get a better look.

"I must say, Kitty, red is your color," Gerry said. Blythe just shook her head. She still couldn't believe someone stole her designs and gave them to Kitty! "And, Priscilla, why would you say Kitty is the perfect pet?"

"Well, just look at her!" Priscilla said. "Isn't she gorgeous? Who wouldn't want a little Kitty Velvet in their life?" The crowd applauded and cheered.

"Everyone seems to agree!" Gerry chirped. "Now we have one last contestant. Blythe, please come back and bring Penny!"

"Are you ready?" Blythe whispered to Penny.

"Yes!" Penny said.

Blythe and Penny walked over to Gerry Geralds. Penny was absolutely glowing in her sapphire-blue outfit. Everyone was oohing and aahing over the adorable panda.

"Well, Blythe, it seems like you might have saved the best for last," Gerry said. "What a cutie Penny is!"

"Yes, she is," Blythe agreed. "Penny is cuddly, loving, and has the biggest heart of all the animals in my pet shop. Everyone loves Penny. She brings joy and happiness wherever she goes. Penny is simply the best!"

At this point, Penny turned to the audience and waved. Everyone started snapping photos with their cell phones! Then Penny turned to Gerry and gave him a huge hug. The audience went crazy!

Gerry smiled and said, "Well...I don't

know what to say except…watch out, Kitty Velvet, you've got some serious competition today!"

In the audience, Priscilla Lee took out her cell phone and made a call. "You didn't tell me about the panda!" she hissed, and hung up.

"Woo-hoo! *Goooo, Penny!*" Zoe cheered.

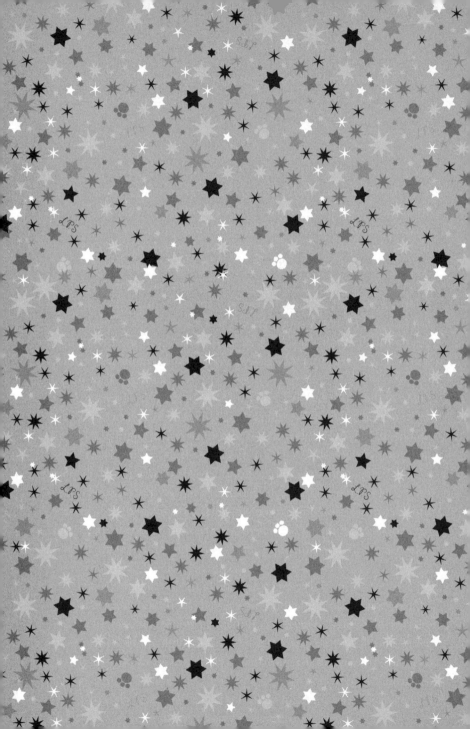

Chapter 15

The next portion of the pageant was talent. There were the usual dogs and puppies rolling over, playing dead, and fetching various objects from their owners. There were parakeets that talked and said funny things that their owners had taught them, and an occasional pet that got stage fright and just ran away.

Blythe gathered her little group together for a pep talk. "Okay, guys, how's everybody feeling?" she asked.

"I feel great!" Russell said.

"Never better," Vinnie replied.

"I'm a bit nervous, but I'll be all right," Sunil said.

"I'm good," Pepper said. "I hope I don't get nervous and you know...stink up the joint. But I wouldn't mind spraying that Gerry Geralds, for a laugh. It would be worth it just to see the look on his face, ha!"

"No, it wouldn't," Blythe said sternly. "Pepper, if you spray someone, the pageant will officially be over. Not to mention the bad publicity for the pet shop. So...please don't!"

"Don't worry, Blythe, it was just a thought," Pepper said with a grin.

"I can't wait to go on!" Minka said, jumping around impatiently. "Am I next?"

At that *very* moment, Zoe and Jack LaLobster appeared. "You all are doing great!" Zoe said. "I'm so proud of you all."

"And the word on the street is the pageant is going to come down to Penny and Kitty Velvet," Jack LaLobster said. "How are you feeling, Penny?"

"I'm...okay, for the most part," Penny said.

Blythe was attaching the scarf made from all the pets' costumes, and her big brimmed hat, which she promised to wear for the talent portion.

"Do I really need to wear all this?" she asked.

"Yes!" Zoe said emphatically. "We said you had to glam it up a bit for the talent portion, remember?"

Blythe led Penny over to a full-length mirror set up for all the pets to review their outfits before performing. "See? You look amazing!" Blythe said.

"I guess," Penny agreed. "It's just so not me...It's more like...*her.*" She happened to glance to her right and see Kitty Velvet being fussed over by two or three different pet handlers. They were fluffing out her fur, touching up her eyelashes, and gushing over her fabulous ruby-red feather boa.

"You are Penny, and she is Kitty," Blythe said. "You each have your own style, which you show in your performance. Don't worry about her. You are going to be great!"

"Thanks, Blythe," Penny said. "Okay... I'm ready, I guess!"

"Fantastic," Blythe said. "Okay, on with the show!"

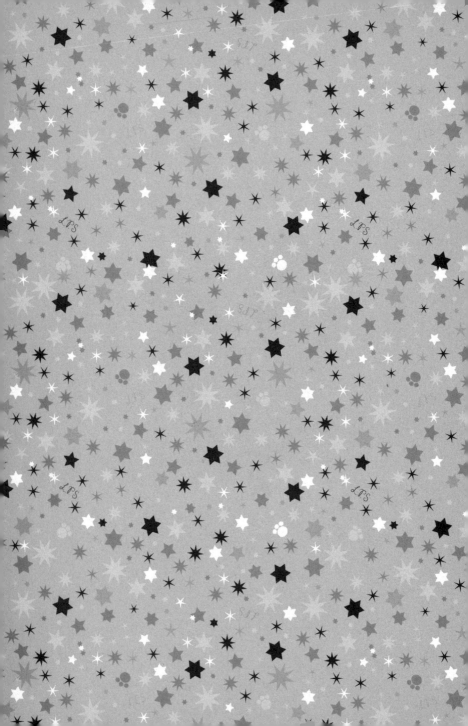

Chapter 16

Sarah was worried about Benny. She'd tried to make him do various cute things for his talent (chase after a fake mouse, sit at a toy piano and pretend to play it), but he would have nothing to do with it. Whenever she said, "What are you going to do for your talent, Benny?" he just started meowing at the top of his lungs. Sarah sighed. "We'll just have to make do," she told Benny. "But I do believe you're going to lose some points in this round."

When Benny's name was announced, Gerry Geralds asked Sarah what Benny was going to do for his talent. "I think he's going to ... sing?" Sarah said.

"Wonderful!" Gerry said. Then he turned to Benny. "Benny, the stage is yours," he said. "Have fun."

Benny walked over to center stage and started meowing. A lot. The people in the audience snickered. But Blythe and the pets heard this:

"Pepper, you are the spice of my life.

Pepper, you make everything nice!

Pepper, how can I make you see that you're the only one for me?

With your fur so dark and your eyes so bright,

You're who I dream of every night!
Pepper, Pepper!
How can I make you see
You're the only one for me?"

Pepper covered her face with her paws in embarrassment.

"Don't be embarrassed," Zoe told her. "I wish someone felt that way about me! That was beautiful!"

"That was a lovely...er...song, Benny," Gerry said. "But you know, I couldn't help but notice Benny kept looking over at Pepper during his song! Maybe he has a crush on the skunk! Wouldn't that be something, folks? We've had pets fall in love during our pageants before, but never a cat and a skunk! That would be one for the record books."

"She...is...not...a skunk!" Benny hissed

at Gerry. But of course he just saw (and heard) a cat hissing at him, and so he quickly backed off.

"Well. Why don't we have Pepper Clark perform next?" Gerry asked. Blythe and Pepper walked to center stage (which was actually the center of the boardwalk, where a small platform has been set up). Blythe gently put down a small keyboard in front of Pepper.

"Pepper plays the piano?" Gerry asked, shocked.

"Indeed she does," Blythe said.

"All right, then," Gerry said. "Pepper Clark on the keyboard, ladies and gentlemen."

Pepper took a deep breath and began playing her opera piece. To all the pets (and Benny and Blythe), it sounded wonderful, but to the audience, it was simply an animal hitting keys with its paws. Still they were entertained and applauded politely.

She's the most wonderful cat in the world, Benny thought to himself with a blissful sigh.

"Next up, we have Sunil Nevla," Gerry announced. Sunil took the stage a bit timidly, and Blythe handed him a small deck of cards.

"Sunil is actually a wonderful magician," Blythe said. "Everyone, meet the amazing Sunil!"

Sunil bowed slightly and received thunderous applause!

"The amazing Sunil needs a volunteer," Blythe continued. "Gerry, would you do the honors?"

"Me?" Gerry exclaimed. "I've always wanted to be part of a magic act! Why, I'd be delighted."

Sunil scattered the playing cards in front of him and looked up at Blythe expectantly.

"He would like you to pick a card," Blythe said. "Any card!"

Gerry picked a card and showed it to the audience. It was the ten of clubs.

Sunil looked down at the deck. Blythe told Gerry to put his card back in the deck.

Sunil tried to shuffle the cards but ended up simply scattering them madly about the stage. He grabbed a card in his mouth and showed it to Gerry. It was not the ten of clubs. Gerry shook his head. Sunil grabbed another, and Gerry smiled and shook his head again. Sunil whispered to Blythe to look behind Gerry's ear, but there was no card there.

"I don't understand. It worked perfectly with Vinnie!" Sunil said. Of course the audience only heard a mongoose chattering, but they were still charmed by Sunil's outfit and the fact that he tried to perform a magic trick. He got a huge round of applause, too.

"Next up is Minka Mark," Gerry said. He smiled as he saw Blythe return with Minka perched on her shoulder. Blythe was also carrying a small paintbrush, white paper, and a can of yellow paint.

"*Ah,* do we have an artist in our midst?" Gerry asked.

"We do!" Blythe said. "Minka would love to paint for you."

Blythe sat Minka down, placed the white paper in front of her, opened the can of paint, and handed Minka the paintbrush. Minka immediately got to work, painting yellow crescents.

"What are those...yellow moons?" Gerry said, peering down. "Oh, wait! I get it! Bananas, of course!" He held up Minka's artwork for everyone to see. Everyone applauded, and someone in the audience actually yelled out, "How much for the painting?"

"I'm sorry, Minka's artwork is not for sale," Blythe replied.

Vinnie was next! Blythe brought Vinnie to the stage and handed him his little paper umbrella. She played the song "Singin' in the Rain" on her cell phone as Vinnie pranced around holding the umbrella. Everyone loved the dancing gecko!

Now it was Russell's turn. "Russell is going to recite a love poem," Blythe told the audience. "And perhaps there is a lovely hedgehog in the audience somewhere that will hear him," she said to Gerry.

"Or maybe a porcupine?" Gerry suggested with a wink.

"I…am…*not*…a porcupine," Russell muttered.

Russell cleared his throat and began reciting a love poem. Of course the audience heard nothing but a hedgehog squealing. But Russell's poem was so sincere it brought Blythe and the other pets close to tears.

"*Aww*, it almost sounds as though he was really trying to say something, doesn't it, folks?" Gerry said to the crowd. "Next up will be the lovely Kitty Velvet!"

Kitty Velvet walked to center stage with her owner, Priscilla Lee.

"And what will Kitty's talent be today?" Gerry asked.

"Kitty will be showcasing some of the

expressions she uses in her modeling," Priscilla said.

"Well, that certainly sounds interesting and different," Gerry said. "The stage is all yours, Kitty and Priscilla!"

"Thank you," Priscilla said. She turned to Kitty. "Kitty, show us *sweet!*" she said.

Kitty gave a heart-melting look and rested her face on her two front paws.

"Awwww..." the audience murmured.

"Next, Kitty, show us *sad,*" Priscilla said. Kitty responded with big, misty eyes about to brim over with tears.

"OMG, I feel like I could cry myself right now," Brittany Biskit whispered to Whittany.

"Now show us *angry!*" Priscilla said. Kitty hissed at the audience and made a scratching gesture with her paw.

"And finally, show us *love,* Kitty!" and

Kitty put a paw to her face and appeared to be blowing the audience a kiss. The audience ate it up and burst into thunderous applause.

"Wow, she's really good," Zoe said to Jack LaLobster. Would Penny be able to compete?

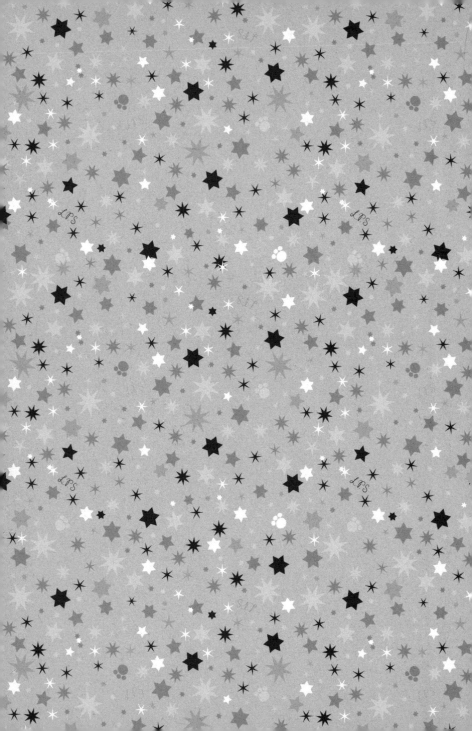

Chapter 17

"And our final contestant is Penny," Gerry said. All the pets huddled together to watch as Blythe brought Penny out to center stage. "What is Penny's talent, Blythe?" Gerry asked.

"Penny is a ribbon dancer," Blythe told him.

"A ribbon dancer!" Gerry repeated. "I can't wait to see that!"

Blythe handed Penny her ribbons, whispered "Good luck!", and stepped back.

Penny began her routine, slowly at first. But right away, Zoe could tell there was a problem.

"Something's wrong," Zoe whispered to LaLobster. "She's not...sparkling at all!"

Zoe was right. Penny wasn't sparkling. It was the fancy scarf. It was the huge hat. It was the silk gloves. It was the makeup on her eyes. She was so uncomfortable and unhappy! She suddenly dropped the ribbons and burst into tears.

"Oh *noooo!*" Zoe moaned.

Blythe was onstage in a flash. She immediately cuddled Penny.

Meanwhile, Priscilla Lee looked down at Kitty Velvet in her arms. "I think a certain kitty is going home with a tiara tonight!"

she whispered happily. Kitty purred in agreement.

Gerry Geralds was uncertain what to do. "Blythe, does Penny want to forfeit the talent portion?" he asked.

"No, no, please!" Blythe begged. "Just give me a minute." She stared at Penny, who had stopped weeping but was now sniffling.

"Penny, you don't have to wear anything you don't want to," Blythe told her. "I'm sorry we tried to make you a glamour girl— even for just a little while! You go out there and just be Penny—and I promise you that will be more than special enough!"

Penny walked out to center stage and began her routine again. First, she took off the long silk gloves. Then the scarf that was both itchy and hot around her neck. Finally, she tossed the beach hat aside. As pretty as it was, it was heavy and making her feel dizzy. But as she tossed the hat, a couple of the shiny balls filled with seashells bounced off the hat. Without even thinking about it, Penny reached out to catch them before they fell to the ground. They were so pretty, Penny thought, it would be a shame if they broke! Without even realizing what she was doing, she started juggling them a bit! The audience applauded. Then Penny put the balls down and began her ribbon-dancing routine.

Freed from the itchy scarf, gloves, and hat, Penny was in the zone. She was twirling her beautiful multicolored ribbons, faster and faster.

"It looks like she's creating a rainbow!" Mrs. Twombly gasped.

Penny was glowing with happiness! She never looked more beautiful.

"Pen-ny Ling! Pen-ny Ling! Pen-ny Ling!"
the audience cheered.

As Penny finished her routine, the audience gave her a standing ovation!

It didn't take the judges long to decide the winner of the Perfect Pet Pageant.

"Was there ever any doubt?" Gerry Geralds asked the audience. "The winner of this year's Perfect Pet Pageant is Miss Penny!"

"YESSSS!!!" all the pets cheered as Blythe gave Penny a huge hug.

Blythe whispered in Penny's ear, "I'm so proud of you! I knew you could do it!"

Benny the tomcat found Pepper in the crowd. "My love, I was hoping you would win. But your friend Penny really is a wonderful performer."

"Yes, she is," Pepper replied. But she was thinking hard. How would she ever get

Benny to believe she was not a cat? "Benny, look. You have to believe me when I say—"

Suddenly, a strange look crossed Benny's face. "What is that smell?" he said. And Pepper realized it was Pepper! She was so nervous about talking to Benny, she started to smell...just a little bit.

"My love, is that...you?" Benny asked, slowly walking a bit away from her.

Pepper sighed. "Yes, Benny, it's me."

"So you really are a skunk!" he said in amazement.

Pepper smiled. "Yes I am. But, Benny, I hope we can still be friends?" she asked, remembering Penny's words. *You can never have too many friends.*

"Of course, my love!" Benny replied. "We will always be friends. But right now...

I hope you don't mind, but I have to go." Pepper followed Benny's eyes and saw he was staring at a pretty Persian cat in the crowd. All Pepper could do was shrug and laugh.

"Take care, Benny!" Pepper said. The pets would always be grateful to him that he came through in a pinch for them.

"Attention, please!" Gerry Geralds said. "It's now time to crown our new perfect pet!" He held up a sparkly tiara and placed it on Penny's head. Everyone cheered!

"And now, Miss Penny, we have a special prize, selected especially for you," Gerry said. He handed Penny a large silver platter—piled high with bamboo shoots! "And may I just say, congratu—" But before he could even get the word out, Penny dove face-first into the delicious platter of bamboo and started eating away to her heart's content.

"Woo-hoo! Three cheers for Penny!" Blythe yelled as all the pets laughed and cheered for Penny, natural beauty *and* winner of the Perfect Pet Pageant!

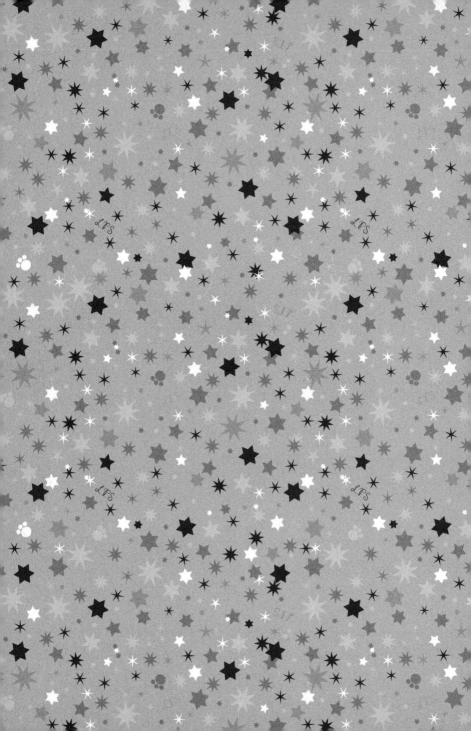